This book
belongs to:

To Vinson Ming-Da, a boy who eats noodles in many different ways!
—Y.C.C.

To Zhou Er Zhuan and Pong Lei.
—Y.X.

ïmmedium

Immedium, Inc.
P.O. Box 31846
San Francisco, CA 94131
www.immedium.com

First hardcover edition published 2002 by Holiday House.
First Immedium hardcover edition published 2016.

Book design by Joy Liu-Trujillo for Swash Design Studio
Chinese translation by Xiaoqing Chen and Carissa Duan

中文审校: 张瀛、邹海燕

Printed in Malaysia
10 9 8 7 6 5 4 3 2 1

Library of Congress Cataloging-in-Publication Data

Compestine, Ying Chang.
The story of noodles / by Ying Chang Compestine; illustrated by YongSheng Xuan.
p. cm.
Summary: Left alone to prepare their family's prize-winning dumplings for the annual cooking contest, the young Kang boys accidentally invent a new dish, "mian tiao," or noodles. Includes a cultural note and a recipe for long-life noodles.
ISBN: 0-8234-1600-3
[1. Noodles—Fiction. 2. Cookery, Chinese—Fiction. 3. Family life—China—Fiction. 4. China—Fiction.]
I. Xuan, YongSheng, ill. II. Title: PZ7.C73615 Su 2002
[E]—dc21
2001059414

ISBN: 978-1-59702-121-0

The Story of Noodles

Noodles

Amazing Chinese Inventions

面条的故事

神奇的中国发明

By **Ying Chang Compestine** · 张瀛/文

Illustrated by **Yongsheng Xuan** · 宣永生/图

Immedium, Inc.   San Francisco

"Stop playing with your food, boys!" scolded Mama Kang. "Remember, a farmer had to sweat for every grain of rice. Pick them all up!"

"孩子们，不要玩你们的食物！" 康妈妈厉声说。"记住，粒粒皆辛苦。把掉下的米粒都捡起来!"

The three Kang boys, Pan, Ting, and Kùai, cleaned up the rice from the floor. Then they started cleaning each other up.

"Ho, Pan," Ting exclaimed. "You have rice in your hair."

"Oh ho, Ting," Pan answered. "You have rice in your ears."

"Oh ho ho, Ting and Pan," Kùai laughed. "You have rice in your toes."

康家兄弟，盼、廷、快，把地上的食物捡起后，开始清理对方身上的米粒。

"嘿，盼，"廷突然说，"你头发上有米粒。"

"哈哈，廷，"盼应道，"你的耳朵里有米粒。"

"噢哈哈，廷、盼，"快笑道，"你们俩的脚趾里有米粒。"

They were still picking up the last few grains when Mama called out, "Time to sleep, boys!"

Once they were in bed, Kùai said to his brothers, "It takes so long to pick up all that rice. We have no time to play."

"I wish we didn't eat rice every day," said Ting.

"What else can we do?" asked Pan. "It's what everyone in China eats."

"孩子们，该睡觉了。"妈妈喊道。这时，康家兄弟还在清理剩下的米粒。

躺下后，快对哥哥们说："我们捡米粒花了那么长的时间，都没有时间玩了。"

"要是我们不每天吃米饭就好了。"廷说。

"我们还能吃什么呢？"盼说，"在中国每个人都吃米饭呢。"

A few days later, Mama announced, "Boys, I need your help for the annual cooking contest."

"Your dumplings will win again," said Ting.

"Maybe Aunt Lee's dumplings will win this year," said Pan.

"We'd better come up with something new," said Kùai.

"But your mother makes the best dumplings," said Papa.

"And this year we're going to make the best ones ever!" said Mama.

几天后，妈妈宣布："儿子们，你们要帮我一起准备一年一度的烹调大赛。"

"您做的饺子肯定又可以赢。"廷说。

"也许李阿姨的饺子今年会赢。"盼说。

"我们今年最好能发明一道新菜。"快说。

"可是你妈妈包的饺子是最棒的呀。"爸爸说。

"今年我们会包出最好的饺子！"妈妈说。

Early the next morning, Mama called out, "Boys, let's get ready for the contest! Pan, grind some wheat in the stone grinder. Papa, start the fire. Ting, get water from the well. Kùai...where is Kùai?"

"He went to feed the pigs," answered Ting.

Suddenly, Kùai ran into the house. "Mama! Papa! I can't find the black pig!"

"Mama, we have to find our pig before it gets into the neighbors' fields again," said Papa.

"Ai yo! What about my dumplings? Boys, stay here. Roll the dumpling wrappers, one at a time. Make sure they are the same size." Papa dragged Mama out the door.

第二天一大早，妈妈喊道：“儿子们，我们现在就为比赛做准备吧。盼，你用石碾磨些麦子。孩子他爸，你去烧火。廷，你从井里打水。快……人哪里去了？”

“他去喂猪了。”廷答道。

突然，快跑进屋子，“爸爸妈妈，我找不到那头黑猪了。”

“孩子他妈，我们要赶快找到那头黑猪呀，要不又闯进邻居家的田里了。”爸爸说。

“哎哟！我的饺子该怎么办呀？”妈妈说，“孩子们，你们留在这里，帮我擀饺子皮，一片一片地擀。要保证擀出的皮都是一样大的。”爸爸拉着妈妈出了门。

"Let's flatten the dough and then cut it with tea cups," said Kùai. "That'll be less work."

"Mama doesn't do it that way," Pan said.

"But my way is easier," said Kùai. The boys lifted the top of the stone grinder and dropped it on the dough. Kùai jumped on top of the grinder and called out. "Come on! Get on top. We need to flatten the dough!"

Ting and Pan climbed up.

"我们先把面团压平，再用茶杯口切出一个个圆形吧。"快建议道。"这样简单些。"

"但是妈妈可不是那样擀皮的呢。"盼说。

"可是我的方法更简单。"快说。男孩们把石碾抬起后压住面团。快跳到石碾上喊道："来吧，你们也跳上来。这样才能够把面团压平！"

廷和盼都爬了上去。

BOOM! BOOM! BOOM!

The table broke. The boys, grinder, dough, and filling flew to the floor. "Ouch, my bottom!" cried Ting.

"We are in big trouble," groaned Pan.

"Stop whining. Let's figure something out before Mama and Papa come back," Kùai urged. "What about…"

砰！砰！砰！

桌子被压垮了。男孩、石碾、面团和饺子馅都翻倒在地上。"噢，我的屁股好痛！"廷喊道。

"我们闯大祸了。"盼哭着说。

"不要发牢骚了。我们要在爸妈回来前想个办法。"
快催促着说，"要不……"

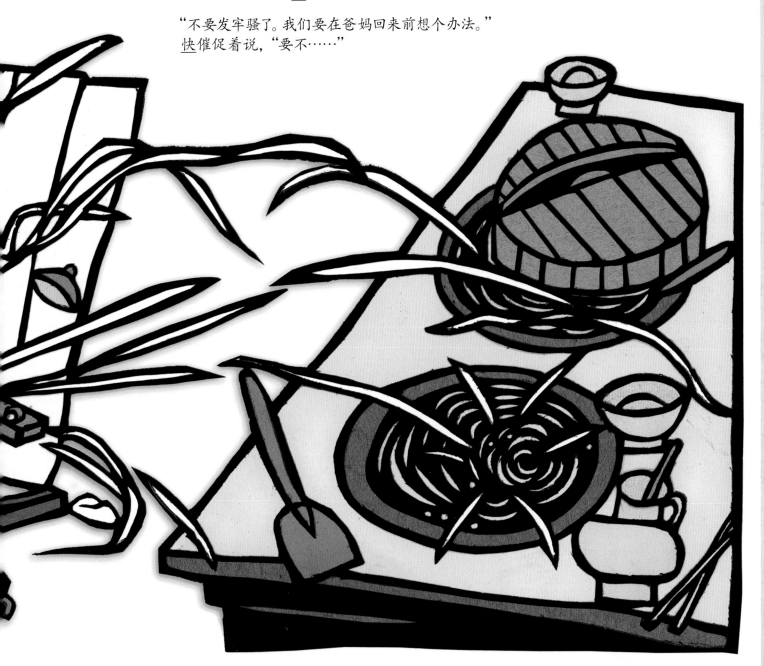

When Mama and Papa returned with the pig, they were surprised by what they saw. "Ai yo! What happened to my dumplings? And my table!" Mama cried.

All the dough was cut into long strips. Some were lying on the broken table. Some were stuck on the wall and furniture while others were still cooking in boiling water. The boys gathered around, eating and slurping.

"What have you done?" asked Papa.

当爸爸妈妈赶着黑猪回来的时候，他们被眼前的一幕惊呆了。妈妈喊道："哎哟，我的饺子和桌子怎么弄成这样了？"

所有的面团都被切成了长条。有些长条摊在压垮的桌面上，有些黏在墙上和家具上，有些则已在滚水里煮着。而那三个男孩则聚在一起，哧溜哧溜地吃着煮好的长条。

爸爸问："你们都干了些什么？"

"Mama and Papa, don't be upset. We invented a new dish! Let me show you how to eat it." Pan rolled the cooked strips around the tip of his chopsticks and stuffed them into his mouth. "This is called 'eating a drumstick.'"

"Watch me!" Ting placed one end of a long strip in his mouth and slurped it up noisily. "This is called, 'sucking a worm.'"

"But I know the best way." Kùai stuffed the long strips into his mouth and bit them off with his teeth. "This is called 'cutting the grass.'"

"爸爸妈妈，不要生气。我们发明了一道新菜。我来告诉你们怎么吃。"盼把长条卷绕在筷子尖上塞入嘴里，说道："这叫'吃鸡腿'。"

"看我的！"廷把长条的一端放入嘴里，然后哧溜一声把它吸入嘴里。说道："这叫'吸蠕虫'。"

"我的吃法最好。"快把很多长条塞入嘴里，并用牙齿把它们咬断。"这叫'切草根'。"

Papa tried hard not to laugh. But Mama wasn't laughing. "Now we have no time to make more dumplings. And you broke my table too."

Kùai chimed in, "We can bring our strips to the contest."

"Yes, yes!" cheered Ting and Pan.

"We don't have much time left," warned Papa. Mama sighed and nodded.

爸爸看到此情形，忍俊不禁。但是妈妈丝毫没有笑意。"现在我们没有时间再包饺子了。你们把我的桌子也压垮了。"

快插话道："我们可以带我们的长条去参加比赛。"

"好，好！"廷和盼欢呼着。

"我们剩下的时间不多了。"爸爸提醒道。妈妈叹着气点了点头。

Everybody cheered when the Kang family arrived. "Did you bring your delicious dumplings?"

"Sorry, we didn't make dumplings this year," Mama said sadly.

"I did, though!" Aunt Lee presented her dish to the judges: the scholar, the king's chef, and the matchmaker.

"Yum! Delicious," praised the judges. Aunt Lee beamed with delight.

当康家人到达赛场时，大家欢呼起来。"你们又带来那美味的饺子了？"

"不好意思，我们今年没包饺子，"妈妈难过地说。

"我可包了饺子，"李阿姨边说边把她的饺子端给了三位评委：智者、御厨和媒人。

"好吃！真是美味。"评委们赞赏道。李阿姨满面春风。

Finally, the scholar called for the Kang family. The villagers crowded around as Mama uncovered her dish. "What's this?" asked the chef.

"You invented it. You tell the judges," Mama said to Kùai.

"These strips are made from dumpling dough," said Kùai.

"How do you eat them?" asked the matchmaker. Each boy quickly grabbed his chopsticks.

最后，智者叫康家人上场。康妈妈端上他们的菜肴，村里人都围了上来。"这是什么？"御厨问。

妈妈对着<u>快</u>说："你发明的这道菜，你来告诉评委吧。"

<u>快</u>说："这些长条是由饺子面团做成的。"

"怎么吃这些长条？"媒人问道。康家三兄弟即刻拿出他们的筷子。

"This is called 'eating a drumstick.'" Pan wound the strips around his chopsticks and stuffed them into his mouth.

"This is called 'sucking the worm.'" Ting slurped one up noisily.

"This is called 'cutting the grass.'" Kùai bit off the strips with his teeth.

All the children pushed closer. "Me, me! Let me try it!"

"这叫'吃鸡腿'。"盼将长条卷绕在筷子尖上塞入嘴里。

"这叫'吸蠕虫'。"廷哧溜将一根长条吸入嘴里。

"这叫'切草根'。"快用牙齿将塞入嘴里的长条咬断。

在场的其他孩子都往前挤, 嚷着: "我! 我! 我也要尝一尝!"

"Quiet! Quiet!" The judges silenced the crowd.

"Why did you invent a new dish?" asked the chef.

"We wanted a food that is easier to clean up after food fights," said Kùai.

"安静！安静！"评委们示意众人安静下来。

"你为什么发明这道菜？"御厨问。

"我们想找一种吃的东西，在食物大战后容易打扫。"快回答道。

The scholar tried "eating a drumstick."
The chef tried "sucking a worm."
The matchmaker tried "cutting the grass."

智者尝试了一口"吃鸡腿"。

御厨尝试了一口"吸蠕虫"。

媒人尝试了一口"切草根"。

The judges gathered and talked quietly.

The crowd murmured, "Do they like it? They praised Aunt Lee's dumplings."

Aunt Lee was peeking under the red silk that covered the big prize sent by the emperor.

评委们聚集在一起，小声地商议着。

众人们也小声嘀咕着："评委们会喜欢吃长条吗？他们已经表扬了李阿姨的饺子啊。"

李阿姨这时候正偷偷瞄着被红丝绸盖着的皇帝送的大奖品。

A long time seemed to pass. Finally, the scholar asked,
"What did you call these strips?"

"Since they are made of flour, we call them *mian tiao* — flour strips,"
Kuai said proudly.

似乎过了很长时间。最后，智者问："这些长条有名字吗？"

快神气地说："这些长条是用面粉做的，所以我们叫它们面条——面做的长条。"

The matchmaker proclaimed, "The Kang family's *mian tiao* are new, delicious, and simple to make. Aunt Lee's dumplings are delicious, but the emperor has already eaten many kinds of dumplings."

The chef revealed the prize. "The emperor sent his best cooking table for the winner: the Kang family!"

媒人向众人说："康家人的面条是道新菜，不仅味道好而且做工简单。李阿姨的饺子是好吃，但是皇帝已经尝过了各种不同的饺子。"

御厨揭开奖品上的红色丝绸，宣布："皇帝把他最好的烹饪桌子赐予本次比赛的冠军——康家。"

The crowd cheered. Mama hugged her three boys. Papa bowed to the judges and the crowd. "Thank you!"

Children gathered around the bowl of *mian tiao* and tried "eating a drumstick," "sucking a worm," and "cutting the grass."

Before long people were eating flour strips in every part of China. From there they spread to other countries, including America, where they are called noodles.

As for the Kang family, sometimes they ate rice; other times they ate noodles.

众人一齐欢呼。康妈妈紧紧抱着自己的三个儿子。康爸爸向评委和众人鞠躬致谢："谢谢你们！"

孩子们聚在面条碗的周围，品尝着"吃鸡腿"、"吸蠕虫"和"切草根"。

不久，中国各地的人们都开始吃面条。后来，面条也传播到了包括美国在内的其他国家。在美国，面条叫"noodles"。

至于康家，他们有时吃米饭，有时吃面条。

When the boys ate rice, they no longer threw it at one another.
But when they ate noodles...

BOOM!

当康家兄弟吃米饭的时候,他们再也不打食物战了。但当他们吃面条的时候……

砰!

Author's Note

Noodles originated in northern China, as early as the first century CE. Chinese historians believe that noodles and cake were mainly an invention of the common people. From China noodles spread throughout Asia.

Around the end of the 13th century, the Italian explorer Marco Polo introduced noodles to Italy, where they were adapted to create the first spaghetti. From Italy they spread throughout the Western world.

Rice and noodles have been the base of many dishes in China. People in northern China eat more noodles than people in the south. Noodles can be cooked in soup, fried, or eaten cold with sauce. They can be served alone or accompanied by meat, eggs, vegetables, or fruit.

Chinese children are taught to roll noodles around the tips of their chopsticks and eat them like a chicken drumstick.

It is the custom in China to make big slurping noises while eating noodles. It is believed that the louder the noise, the more delicious the noodles.

Children are allowed to bite off long noodles with their teeth. Some mothers cut the noodles with scissors before serving them to their children.

作者寄语

面条起源于中国的北方，最早要追溯到公元一世纪。中国历史学家们认为，面条是老百姓发明的，也是从中国传遍到了整个亚洲的。

大约在13世纪末，意大利探险家马可·波罗把面条带到了意大利。在意大利，人们以中国的面条制作方法为基础，发明了意大利面条。由此，面条从意大利传播到整个西方世界。

在中国，米饭和面条一直以来都是主食。中国北方人比南方人更喜欢吃面条。面条有煮、炒、凉拌等多种吃法。人们可以单吃面条，也可以配上肉、鸡蛋、蔬菜或水果一起吃。

中国的孩子们学会了把面条卷绕在筷子尖上吃，这种吃法远看就像是在吃鸡腿。

在中国，人们习惯在吃面条时发出哧溜哧溜的声音。大家认为哧溜声越响，表明面条越好吃。

孩子们吃长面条的时候，可以把面条咬断。有些妈妈们在给孩子吃面条前会先用剪刀把面条剪短。

Long Life Noodles

Makes 4 servings

Ingredients:

- ½ pound cooked fresh or dry noodles (Chinese egg noodles, spaghetti, etc.)

For the sauce:

- 2 green onions, white part only, chopped
- 2 small cloves of garlic, peeled
- ½ cup smooth almond or peanut butter
- ½ cup coconut or soy milk
- 1 tablespoon lemon juice
- 1 tablespoon soy sauce or salt to taste

For the garnish:

- ¼ cup roasted nuts
- ¼ cup dried cranberries

Directions:

1. With the help of an adult, chop the green onions and combine all sauce ingredients in a blender or food processor. Blend until smooth.

2. In a big bowl, toss the noodles with the sauce. Garnish with nuts and cranberries. Serve cold.

3. You can substitute other fruit for the cranberries. Try raisins, grapes, or fresh berries.

长寿面
四人份

用料:
- ½ 磅煮好的新鲜面或干面 (中国式鸡蛋面、意大利面, 等等)

调料:
- 2 根青葱, 只取葱白, 切碎
- 2 个小的大蒜头, 去皮
- ½ 杯杏仁酱或花生酱
- ½ 杯椰奶或豆奶
- 1 汤匙柠檬汁
- 1 汤匙酱油或盐末 (自行调味用)

装饰料:
- ¼ 杯烤好的坚果
- ¼ 杯蔓越莓干

做法:
1. 在家长的帮助下, 将青葱切碎, 并把所有的调味料都放入搅拌机或食品加工机中搅拌, 直至混合均匀。
2. 在大碗中将面条和调味料搅拌均匀。在面条上放上坚果和蔓越莓做装饰。无需加热。
3. 你可以用其它水果代替蔓越莓, 比如葡萄干、葡萄或新鲜的莓类。

Enjoy more adventures by the Author!

"Bold and beautiful cut-paper design in bright colors, resembling stained glass, instantly draws our attention. Popular Chinese-American author Ying Chang Compestine cooks up a tale to let children in on the birth of chopsticks."

— In Culture Parent

"...the brothers' reversal from troublemakers to heroes will appeal to many young people, as will Xuan's colorful, expertly crafted cut-paper illustrations."

— ALA Booklist

"...the playfulness and creativity of the Kang brothers make this... especially appealing."

— School Library Journal

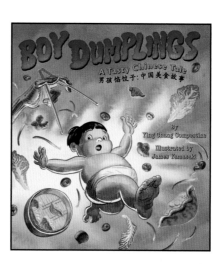

"...a classic trickster tale, developing both characters and premise with humor."

— Kirkus Reviews